Acknowledgments

The author and designer wish to thank Fathers Bernardino Bucci and Robert Young, OFM;
Tom Fahy's Center for the Divine Will; the Canonical Pious Association of Luisa Piccarreta;
Joseph Bolognino for his ever-generous, multi-faceted assistance;
Robert (Rob-bayl) Ketcham and Lachlan Cameron, for finding the fly in the ointment.

The illustrator would like to acknowledge the world-famous artists whose work had already
treated of the subjects in this universal story, and whose wonderful masterpieces she has referenced:
the Italians, Leonardo da Vinci and Michelangelo Buonarrotti,
the Dutch, Johannes Vermeer, and the Hungarian, M.S. Mester.

Gingerbread House

602 Montauk Highway
Westhampton Beach
New York 11978 USA

SAN: 217-0760

Visit us at
GingerbreadBooks.com

Edited by Josephine Nobisso and Maria Nicotra

Art Direction and Design by Maria Nicotra and Josephine Nobisso

The illustrations were created in acrylic on canvas, and collage.

Manufactured by Regent Publishing Services Limited
Printed in China

FIRST EDITION
10 9 8 7 6 5 4 3 2 1

Library of Congress Cataloging-in-Publication Data

Nobisso, Josephine.
Take It to the Queen: A Tale of Hope / Josephine Nobisso; illustrated by Katalin Szegedi. -- 1st ed.
    p. cm.
Summary: Although favored by their king, his charitable wife, and their peace-loving son, ungrateful
villagers turn away and bring disaster upon themselves, then, when they have nothing left, repent
and ask the queen to intervene on their behalf. Includes an explanation of the religious bases of the
story and an explanation of the symbolism therein.
ISBN 978-0-940112-19-3 (hardcover) -- ISBN 978-0-940112-21-6 (paperback)
[1. Conduct of life--Fiction. 2. Kings, queens, rulers, etc.--Fiction. 3. Christian life--Fiction. 4. Allegories.]
I. Szegedi, Katalin, 1963- ill. II. Title.
PZ7.N6645 Tak 2008
[Fic]--dc22

2007047019

Josephine Nobisso

TAKE IT TO THE QUEEN

A Tale of Hope

Illustrated by
Katalin Szegedi

Gingerbread House
Westhampton Beach, New York

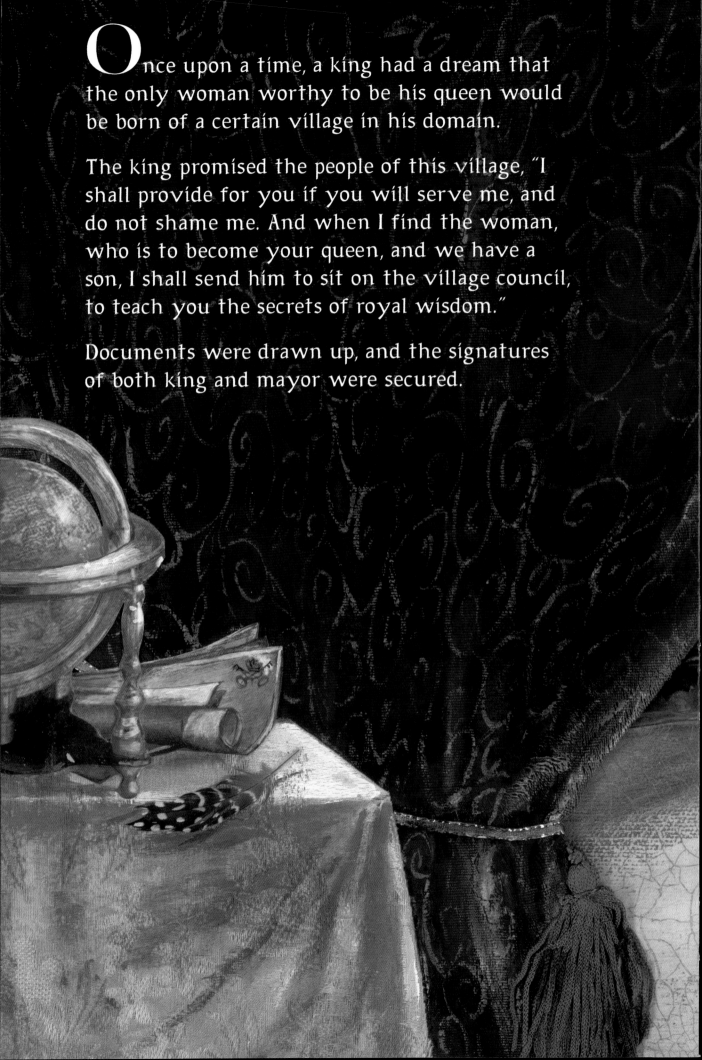

O nce upon a time, a king had a dream that
the only woman worthy to be his queen would
be born of a certain village in his domain.

The king promised the people of this village, "I
shall provide for you if you will serve me, and
do not shame me. And when I find the woman,
who is to become your queen, and we have a
son, I shall send him to sit on the village council,
to teach you the secrets of royal wisdom."

Documents were drawn up, and the signatures
of both king and mayor were secured.

Faithful to his word, the king saw to everything for the villagers. He built a bridge so that they would not have to descend into the dark valley. He erected an aqueduct to bring them clear water. He set aside the largest timbers for their buildings, and he bred fine foals for their stables.

The king reserved the choicest seeds for them, so that their bread baked up rich and fragrant, and their fruits grew ripe with nectar. He routed the finest canvases, parchment, and marble to them, so that those who yearned to, could use their talents.

The king sent gold faucets for their fountain.
The children drank from that gold, horses bent their
necks to its overflow, women wrung wash in its reflection,
and travelers refreshed themselves in the king's generosity.

The villagers lived just as the king willed, and in that conformity,
they found perfect safety and joy.

By and by, the finest girl was, indeed, born in that village. As she grew, she never carried wood without filling the baskets of weaker neighbors. She never baked without laying out loaves for others. And although death took her parents, she always denied herself some pleasure so that she might bestow it upon others.

Ecce ancilla L

One day, as this maiden dozed under an arbor where doves cooed, she herself experienced a remarkable dream. An angel approached, bearing a noble son whose flesh glowed, and whose glance pierced her heart with both sorrow and joy. When the girl awoke, she found the king before her, asking for her hand. "Your wish," she told him, "has always been my own, and always will be."

They were wed, and the entire kingdom rejoiced, especially the favored villagers, for now, they looked forward to the day when a prince would sit among them.

The queen went about the kingdom, bread for the hungry and roses for the weary tucked into her mantle. She helped newborns enter the world, and cradled the aged leaving it. On her tongue, all found kindly counsel. And whenever anyone had a need, the cry resounded, "Take it to the queen!" for the king, cherishing his spouse's virtues, and recognizing his own will and likeness in her, could refuse her no request.

Despite their monarchs' faithfulness, the people of the favored village grew tired of waiting for a prince. Because they labored, they took to believing that they owed nothing to the crown. And because they knew that the prince would be one of their own, they imagined that they had merited the king's extravagances. They neglected their duties until their water ran brown, and their harvests fell to the ants. They charged a toll over the bridge, and they replaced the gold faucets with those of bronze, cheating one another as the objects changed hands.

The king, being justice itself, sent a messenger to the villagers. They had broken their pact, and he could no longer favor them as he would have liked. But because he was also mercy itself, he would remember his promise to one day send his son.

One night, the villagers gawked at fireworks issuing from the castle. Because their charity had grown so cold, and their reason so dim, they barely cared or comprehended that the promised child now was born to them.

As the prince grew, his parents pondered his grace, and they were well pleased. The royal court delighted in announcing, "Behold! The Prince of Peace!"

In the fullness of time, the king sent the boy and his mother to the queen's village, to bring the people to their senses.

Some few villagers felt their hearts swell and quicken with new hope at the approach of these monarchs, so good and so kind.

But, instead of giving the prince his rightful seat on the village council, a mob spirited away his fine horse, and ransacked his rich saddle. They beat him with the branches of the very trees his father had planted and, as a final insult, they threw the battered sovereign over a donkey that the mayor himself sent off with a kick.

The secret admirers of the sorrowful mother helped her gather her bruised son, to return him to his father.

The king tenderly received the prince, and lamented, "Willful creatures! How they abuse their freedom and bring disaster upon themselves!"

In their goodness, the king, the prince, and the queen were all of one mind and spirit, longing for a gesture of repentance so that the villagers might be restored to safety, and so that the peace of the entire kingdom might again be complete.

The terrible day dawned when the villagers found themselves not only with nothing to eat, and no water fit to drink, but also with hearts roiling in suspicion and hatred. The bridge had crumbled, and they had sold their horses for bread, now long gone. No one knew in whose louse-ridden mattress or in which dark hole the gold faucets had been hidden. Their talk turned to nothing other than the days when they used to have everything, and some of it went so far as to blame their misfortune on the king.

Rebellion welled up, but the queen's cohort argued, "The king still offers us everything! But how can he give it, if we withhold allegiance from him, and affection from his queen?" The villagers then urged the mayor, "Go to the castle! Take our plight to the queen, who is, after all, one of us! Ask her to beg the king's mercy, not only because we and our children are about to die of wretchedness, but because we are sorry for the way we abused the prince, and because our monarchs are good, and deserving of all our love!"

The villagers searched for a peace offering. Finally they plucked the one fruit that remained to them—an apple, small and deformed, with a wormhole through its skin.

The queen received her neighbor with solicitude. With great joy she heard of the villagers' change of heart. The mayor told her, "We have reduced ourselves to nothing but this rotting apple. I fear it will offend the king whom we have already too much offended. We are not worthy to approach him ourselves, and so we beg you to intercede on our behalf."

The queen carried the apple into the royal chambers. And as she related all she had learned from the mayor, she handed it to her son, who regarded it, and passed it to his father. The king halved the fruit, and carved away its decaying flesh. He removed its worm, and peeled its blemished skin. He then returned it to the prince, who sliced the offering into wafer-thin wedges.

With her own hands, the queen arranged the fruit on a golden platter. She finished her account with the request that the king grant an audience to her penitent neighbor who had treated their son with contempt. The prince himself urged his father to accept the request of so tender a mother, and to offer the poor mayor some of the apple, now transformed into a delectable delight.

With joyful hearts, the villagers welcomed the prince to preside over the village council. He taught them the secrets of royal wisdom. The water in their aqueduct ran clean again, and the bridge was rebuilt.

Sturdy foals once again pranced in the hills above the village. Grain soon overflowed from the storage chests. Luscious fruit ripened in the orchards. And the villagers returned to their peaceful pursuits.

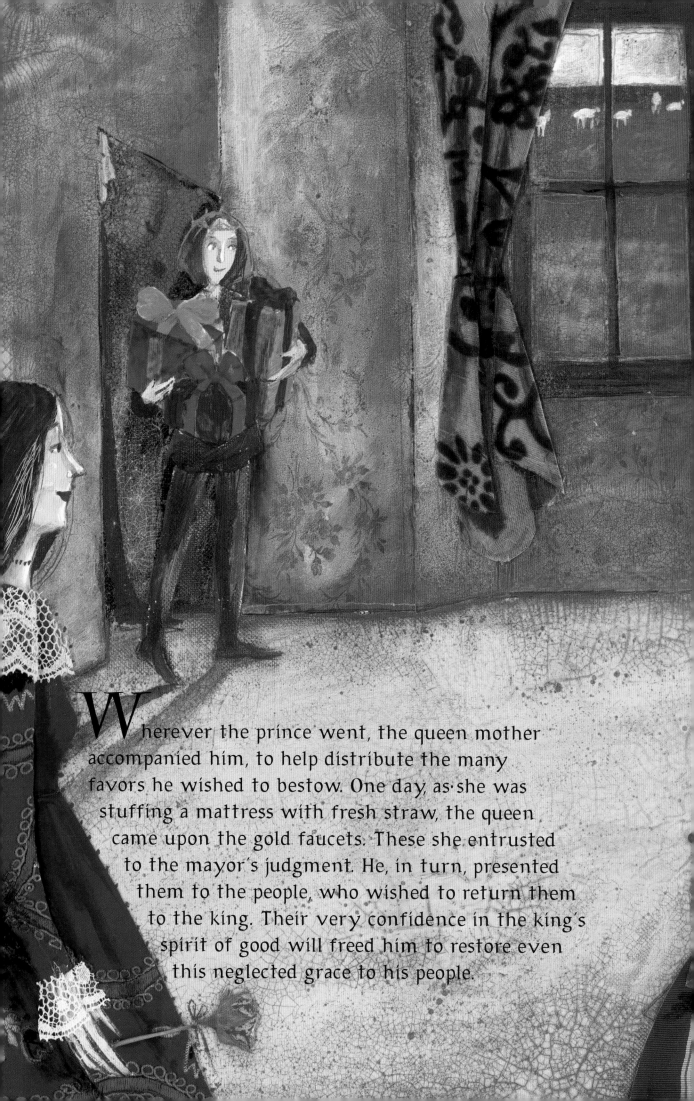

Wherever the prince went, the queen mother accompanied him, to help distribute the many favors he wished to bestow. One day, as she was stuffing a mattress with fresh straw, the queen came upon the gold faucets. These she entrusted to the mayor's judgment. He, in turn, presented them to the people, who wished to return them to the king. Their very confidence in the king's spirit of good will freed him to restore even this neglected grace to his people.

Once again, children bathed in the gold of their king's favor, horses bent to its nourishment, and women wrung their wash in its purity. And the villagers never tired of telling travelers —who refreshed themselves without price— the good news that what they were enjoying was not simply water, but the unfathomable mercy that had been shown to their village—a village that had taken everything to the queen.

Author's Postscript

This fable honors the august role of The Blessed Virgin Mary in salvation. An allegory that takes liberties with eternity by criss-crossing the three eras of history—Creation, Redemption, and Sanctification—it is inspired by my reading and translating the works of the Italian mystic, Luisa Piccarreta, "The Little Daughter of the Divine Will." Through Luisa's volumes, Jesus explains the eventual restoration of man to the order, the place, and the purpose for which he was created.

We creatures are *like* God because of our capacity to possess His virtues. Made *in the image* of God, man is given intellect, memory, and free will with which to cooperate with grace in forming himself. God's very essence, all holy, and all perfect, is His Divine Will. Everything that *is*, seen and unseen, flows from It. The human will remains the most endowed of all our attributes, too, since it is made in the image of the Divine one. It, too, can make things "happen,"—even to choosing to let evil into the world.

Since Adam and Eve's original attributes were not dimmed, as ours became, the just consequences of their trespass had to equal the value of those attributes. Since children cannot inherit goods their parents lose, the just yet merciful Father revealed the remedy at The Fall: He would send "The Woman," from whom the Christ would derive His humanity. Redemption is wrought only with sacrifice, and only the blood of the Creator of blood carries the necessary worth for the ransom to buy back all that our first parents lost.

Although Mary is a creature of the Creator, and possesses a human will from her conception, she eternally sacrifices that will to God, maintaining herself in the blessed state our first parents used to enjoy: she lives in the Kingdom of the Divine Will. God's most fulfilled creature, Our Lady most reflects His image and likeness. Like the queen in our story, The Blessed Mother cooperates in various and essential ways in the ongoing salvific action of her race, assuming the royal roles of Advocate and Mediatrix.[†]

Jesus taught us only one prayer. He would not have asked us to pray for things that cannot be fulfilled. We await the Kingdom, when God's Will will be done on Earth, as it is in Heaven, and we look to Mary as our model and our hope.

Take it to the Queen!

[†] Catechism of the Catholic Church 969

Dedications

For Don Lyon, who unwrapped for me the gift of
Luisa Piccarreta's *The Book of Heaven*,
and for my daughter Maria Nicotra,
my sister Mary (Suzy) Golfo, and our prayer group
who all accompany me through the volumes. -JN

For my parents. -KSz